I Don't Belong Here

Written By
Lynsey Ramsay

Illustrated By
Aileen Falconer

Grosvenor House
Publishing Limited

This book is published by
Grosvenor House Publishing Ltd
Link House
140 The Broadway, Tolworth, Surrey, KT6 7HT.
www.grosvenorhousepublishing.co.uk

A CIP record for this book
is available from the British Library

ISBN 978-1-83975-962-8

In memory of my late partner Ross and also dedicated
to my husband David, as well as my children
Jack, Megan, Charlie and Ava

xxxxxx

"Sometimes, we think we want to disappear when all we really want is to be found."

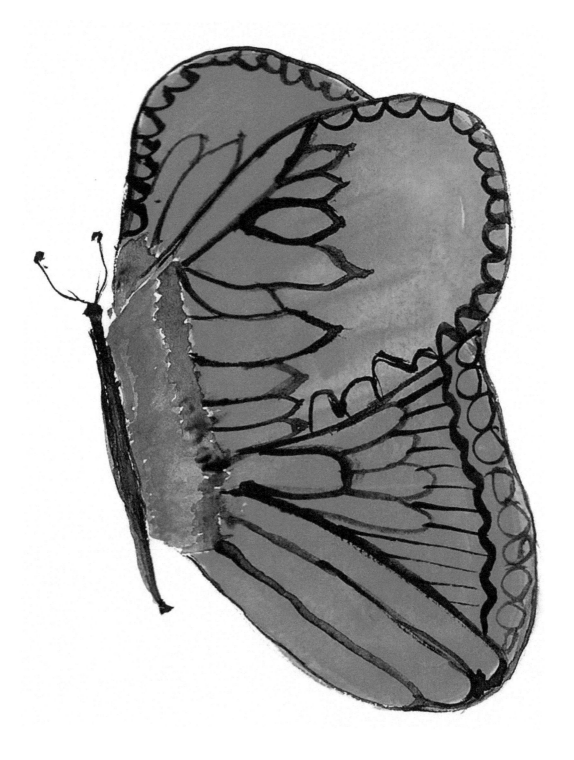

Chapter 1
The Root Chakra - Earth Element
"The Soil where we plant our seeds to grow"

This is the story of a little bear named Willow.

Willow's dad died when he was a small bear, and he would often feel sad and alone.

"Do you know what depression is?" he asked his best friend (his pet caterpillar). "I didn't think you would," said Willow, after he received no reply.

This happened a lot when Willow asked his caterpillar questions.

He spent a great deal of time in his bedroom, with only his caterpillar to talk to.

Since his dad's death Willow had struggled to understand his thoughts and feelings, making it hard for him to make friends.

His family tried to help him but it felt safer to push them away.

He felt lost and like he no longer had the right parts to fit into the world around him, and the parts he did have often ached and felt painful.

The parts he needed were missing and he didn't know where to find them.

Willow's dad died from an illness called depression and Willow often worried that he was ill just like his dad.

"Do you think I have depression?" he asked his caterpillar. "Mum says depression is an illness that affects your mind, and my head hurts sometimes from always thinking. I wonder if I am going to die?"

Often, he would lie awake at night talking to his caterpillar about his worries, but his caterpillar never answered him.

This made going to school hard for Willow as he spent his days asleep and his nights awake.

"I wish I was normal and could fit in with everyone else."

He would often say this, but also liked it being just him and his caterpillar.

He trusted his caterpillar and he knew that he would never leave him. He was the only person he trusted in the world.

"What happens when we die?" he asked, knowing his caterpillar wouldn't answer, but he never gave up hope that one day that his caterpillar would speak to him.

One night, as he was talking over his worries with his caterpillar, he glanced at his bedside clock, the time was 11.11pm. Numbers fascinated Willow especially the number 11. When the numbers appeared like this, it felt like time was stood still. He wasn't sure what it meant, but the voices he often heard in his mind told him there was a reason these numbers kept appearing, but he didn't understand.

He lay there for a bit looking at the clock and then decided he couldn't take any more of the thoughts that he couldn't find the answers to.

"I don't belong here anymore," he said to his caterpillar, as he placed him safely back into his little container.

Willow decided he would leave the life he had in search of what he was missing. He was sure there was something out there that would give him back his old feelings of happiness and safety.

Something to put him back together and become the bear he used to be.

In the silence of the night Willow quietly packed his belongings, picked up his caterpillar, placed a note under his pillow and slipped out the door.

"I'm sorry, I love you all," he whispered, as the door closed behind him.

It was dark and late when he left but that didn't frighten him. He always felt scared and alone; besides he had his caterpillar.

He felt relieved that he had a plan to escape and find what he was looking for.

Chapter 2
Sacral Chakra - Water Element
"The water that helps the seeds to grow"

Shortly after he began his journey the relief he felt began to fade, he realised he didn't know where he was going or what it was he was actually searching for. The smell in the air changed, darkness became deeper and nothing was familiar. He felt completely lost.

"Don't worry," he said to his caterpillar, "I will look after you. I know how scared you are so trust me that I will keep you safe."

Willow tried to hide his own feelings from the caterpillar. He wanted to protect him.

Willow quickly realised how afraid and alone he really was now. He wished he could find his way back. He was completely lost in the deep dark night and in a place he didn't know, but he was trying to be brave for his caterpillar.

"Where am I and how do we get back?" he asked his mind. His mind was always full of chatter so he thought he would try asking his mind instead of frightening his caterpillar. He knew how it felt to be scared so he didn't want his caterpillar to ever feel like he did.

He began to panic, looking in every direction for some light or guidance to help him, but nothing appeared until he caught a glimpse of the full moon in the distance between some tree branches high above.

Exhausted and afraid he decided to trust the light of the moon, and as he bravely took several steps forward he noticed that the moon's light began to shine brighter and fuller.

"The moon is guiding us, we are going to be ok," he said to his caterpillar.

This encouraged him to trust more and so he moved further forwards.

Rain began to fall and Willow realised he needed to find some shelter; in the light of the moon a tree was calling to him. The Weeping Willow Tree stood alone in the light with its bare branches looking sad and fragile as if calling him from within; as Willow got closer, he noticed the raindrops hanging from the branches. He stood before the tree in silence, the raindrops looked like his tears falling. It was as if they knew how each other felt from within. With nowhere else to turn he decided to trust in the callings and take some shelter from the stooping branches of the tree.

He placed his caterpillar down and rested his weary head on his bag, he was exhausted. As he lay down, gazing up towards the sky, the raindrops from the branches fell upon him, connecting with his teardrops, and the tree and Willow cried together. Willow began to realise he could hear his heart beating, this had never happened before, normally it was his mind he heard or his heart racing, but this was a beat and it warmed his heart. As the teardrops fell together Willow searched for some kind of sign to let him know he was going to be ok.

As he searched he realised he hadn't called out to his dad before. His mum always told him his dad had never truly left him and that his soul lived on in their hearts, but Willow didn't understand this either.

He had felt angry at his mum because she couldn't bring his dad back, and he questioned if his dad had really loved him like his mum always told him.

"If you loved me dad, why did you leave me?"

He began to search the sky for his dad. His mum had told him heaven was in the sky but Willow could never understand this as he often looked but he couldn't see heaven. Maybe tonight he would see heaven he thought.

"Where are you dad? I need you."

After a few minutes Willow gave up hope of being heard by his dad and turned away from the moonlight sky on to his side and faced the darkness once again; suddenly the branches of the tree lowered and lifted him. Willow fell into the softness of the branch like a big fluffy cloud. He fell asleep, as he always did, believing that he wasn't good enough to be loved. The light had now faded and darkness had returned. The deep dark night of the forest was pulling him in. Even though he was afraid he felt it was best to stay where he was, as moving anywhere was even more frightening.

When Willow awakened the next morning, he felt different as he lay cradled in the safety of the branch. It had been so long since he had shared a hug and he realised he was not only missing his dad but his mum too. He began to feel guilty as he thought of both his mum and dad. His mum always tried to get close enough to hug Willow but his confused feelings inside meant he pushed her away, and now he began to question if his anger was pushing everyone away, including signs from his dad. He began to realise how much he wanted to be hugged.

Chapter 3
Solar Plexus Chakra - Fire Element
"The Sun that warms the seeds to grow"

As he stirred properly and wiped away his weepy eyes he looked towards the sky, hopeful that he would see some sort of sign, but there was nothing to be seen except dark clouds and bare branches from the tree that seemed to be hopeful too of some light. It had been a long winter for the forest and it seemed as though he wasn't the only one seeking brighter days.

He glanced down at the ground and realised his caterpillar container was open and his caterpillar was gone. His heart sank; he had the same feeling he had when his dad died. He wanted more than anything for this not to be true.

He felt upset and betrayed as he had trusted his caterpillar. The caterpillar knew his deepest thoughts.

"Why would you do this to me?" he asked through tears. "You have left me all alone just like my dad did." Not only did he have no one replying to his questions but now he had no one listening to them either.

He really was all alone in a strange place, unsure where to turn or what to do. He continued to cry.

With no one to talk to he turned to the only thing that never left him alone, the voices inside his head.

"Why can't no one love me?"

"Because you aren't good enough," they said. "You are unlovable and you aren't perfect like everyone else."

Willow held his head in his paws sobbing. "I know this to be true because everyone I love leaves me; I really am so damaged that people cannot love me."

As he sat there wiping his tears and trying to think of another way to escape his sad feelings, he felt a breeze above his head and looked up and saw the bare branches of the trees begin to move as if parting a gap in the sky. In the next moment the rain stopped and the sky became the brightest blue with white fluffy clouds passing by as they began to form a shape. He looked with intrigue as he wiped his tears and opened his eyes wider.

He could see an elephant in the clouds; it was the most beautiful elephant he had ever seen. The trees moved further apart and the elephant grew larger and the white became the brightest light he had ever seen.

Since his dad had died all Willow felt and saw was darkness closing in around him, so the light began to overwhelm him and he felt dizzy. He fell to his knees. His heart was beating fast and loud again and his body felt tingly.

He thought to himself, "This is it, I am where I am meant to be. I am dying." He closed his eyes and waited for something to happen. He didn't know what happens when you die so he didn't know what to expect. He waited anxiously, but again nothing happened. He began to slowly open his eyes apprehensively as to what would be waiting for him.

As his gaze lifted from the ground he saw something float down before him. He reached out and caught the whitest feather.

Willow sat gazing at the feather, he began to hear his heart beating again and felt a strong connection to his dad. He couldn't explain it or understand it but he felt his dad around him. He looked up to the sky but the elephant was gone, as was the blue sky, but he wasn't sad as he knew this was a message from his dad. He looked up to the Willow tree branches and whispered "Thank you."

As he sat cupping his feather in his paws he sensed a gentle presence and looked to find a humming bird sipping water from a white lotus flower in a small Lily Pond that he didn't recall being there before.

"Ahhhh so you received your feather then, how marvellous!" the humming bird said as she looked up towards Willow.

"Who are you and how do you know about my feather?" asked Willow.

"I am the messenger of the forest and I listen deeply, some even say I bring messages from heaven."

The humming bird swiftly flew from the lotus flower she was on to sit with Willow and listen more closely.

"What brings you here bear?" she asked as she placed a brown crystal in Willow's paw.

"I am looking for the missing piece of me to put me back together. All I know is I don't belong where I was before coming here, and now I am lost and feel scared not knowing where I am going."

The humming bird replied, "It's ok to feel scared and unsure, sometimes we need to feel this to find our way, now hold on to your stone as it will protect and help you feel safe. The elephant in the clouds earlier brought you a message of unconditional love and hope with your feather. It's a message from your dad."

Chapter 4
The Heart Chakra - Air Element
"The wind that blows to allow the seeds to grow"

Willow's heart warmed again and he began to feel hungry, he hadn't eaten since he had left home, but this often happened when Willow was sad, he would sometimes forget to eat and other times chose not to eat. He reached into his bag and brought out some bread to share with the bird.

"Thank you for being so kind and sharing with me, it's been a long winter and I too have been afraid, hungry and alone at times," said the bird.

Willow lowered his gaze to the ground feeling ashamed, and again his tears began to fall, "But I am not kind you see. I get angry and do things that are hurtful to others."

The bird moved in closer again and hovered almost as if still under Willow's chin, catching his tears as they dissolved into the soft healing feathers of her wing.

"You have been kind and shared your bread with me. It doesn't matter to me about things you have done before we met. All that matters is the here and now, and to me you have been nothing but kind." The bird flew back to the Lotus flower. "Focus on this beautiful flower before you, she is here to remind you that your wishes are coming true. I am here to connect you with the unconditional love that will always protect you."

The sky around them began to turn the brightest green and Willow could feel the warmth in his heart as it began to open up, just like the petals of the Lotus flower. For the first time in a very long time, he remembered how love felt instead of pain in his heart.

Willow smiled and held his paws close to his heart and whispered to the bird, "Thank you."

"Now that we have connected properly it's time for us to walk together on your journey where you will find the longing you wish for, you will find where you belong." Then the bird flew to another tree. "Follow me," she said, guiding him with her beautiful wings.

There was a very different feel to this tree. It was an oak tree and the magic instantly shone through from between the ivy covered bark of the tree. Willow could feel the wisdom from the tree as its roots connected deep within the earth of the forest.

He began to hear the echo of a voice from within the tree, "Understand who you are not, then you will find who you really are."

With the humming bird on his shoulder, he saw a small doorway carved into the tree; it was too small for him to fit through he thought, but the humming bird reassured him it was sprinkled with the magic of the forest fairies. "All you have to do is close your eyes and believe."

Willow closed his eyes and stepped into the doorway and began to connect with the sound of his heartbeat again, which was shortly followed by the sound of a drum beat from below the tree. A soft light began to shine and Willow realised he was at the top of a stone staircase... he began to take a few steps downwards, feeling his heartbeat and drumbeat become one, just like the raindrops and tear dops under the Weeping Willow Tree.

"But wait," he said, as he stopped in his tracks, "I need to wait for my caterpillar, he might come back for me and I will be gone, and then he will be sad."

"Your caterpillar isn't coming back Willow. It's hard to accept but sometimes whilst searching we lose people we love. We have to disconnect," said the bird, as she guided him once more with her wings, dropping another coloured stone in his paw, this time an orange crystal stone. "This stone will help you trust in our adventure and what you are about to find."

As guilty as he felt, he knew the bird was speaking the truth so he decided to trust her guidance and again felt the beat run through his body, guiding him deeper down inside the tree.

When he reached the foot of the stairwell he was met with another doorway, apprehensive, he slowly began to open the door, the drum beat became louder and Willow became more trusting. Something magical was overwhelming his body and he felt safe. With the warmth of the sun beating against his skin he could smell the sweet smell of moss on the trees. The sound of birds all around was absolutely delightful to his ears. He began to feel the earth below coming up through his body. The different smells and sounds completely warmed his heart, and somewhere nearby he could hear the flow of a river. Everything felt familiar, he felt like he was home.

Not far from where he stood, he could hear water and then saw a small pond, pure clear and still. Another lotus flower floated by, only this time it was indigo colour.

The humming bird delivered Willow's next message with a yellow stone. "This is the place where you will find what you are searching for but to allow this we must still your mind to allow you to see and hear beyond what is before you. Awaiting you between the trees of this forest are messages and lessons for you as part of your journey here. The energy here will help take away your fear and connect you with your intuition."

"I don't understand," said Willow. "What is intuition?"

"Intuition my dear is the voice inside your head, but to hear it properly and to allow it to guide you safely you must let go of your voice of fear," said the humming bird. "Surrender and trust within this world and what you desire will become yours. Be seated now, be still and wait patiently," she said, as she hovered gently by Willow's side.

Willow listened and sat waiting with anticipation for what was to come.

Before long he heard some movement between the long blades of grass, he was excited to see what or who was going to help him find his missing piece. He jumped up to greet them. "Be still," said the bird, "for we need to be patient. We cannot rush or be intrusive on our forest friend for they too have a story."

Willow sat back down to patiently wait, then the bird gave Willow a pink stone. "This is your stone to help you love and to connect with others from your heart to theirs." Before he knew it a turtle appeared. Willow could see the sadness in his eyes. He knew things about others before they even spoke and he knew the turtle carried some of the feelings he had. He decided to wait until the turtle trusted him enough to pull in closer and lay beside Willow.

The turtle had been hurt in the past by his family and found it difficult to find his voice as he was always told to keep secrets, and just like Willow he didn't feel he belonged in the world around him.

"We don't need to share our stories," said Willow, "we can just be here together in this moment with each other."

The tortoise wasn't used to having friends because he found it hard to trust and to speak to others. But that didn't matter to Willow. They didn't have to speak, they understood each other without words.

"Thank you," whispered the tortoise.

Willow was beginning to see his own kindness from within as well as in others. It felt good not to be angry all the time.

Willow, the tortoise and the humming bird sat together basking in the yellow pillar of sunshine and drinking from the cleansing water of the 'Lotus flower; it was a wonderful feeling to just be. As the sun shone the humming bird delivered another message to Willow " Be your own kind of sunshine, to be at one with yourself, embracing the kind and loving person you are."

Before long they felt another presence with them and they looked up to see a dragonfly hovering above them.

"Help me please," she said "for I am lost. I get confused and forget things and I am trying to get home."

"What's your name?" asked Willow.

The dragonfly lowered herself further down to the animals, "I don't know my name, I try to remember but I just can't."

Willow recognised just how deeply he was understanding and feeling the same feelings of the other animals, and that their language was an unspoken one. This happened to him in groups with his friends and it sometimes made things difficult for Willow as he couldn't relax like everyone else. But here in the forest he felt at ease with this knowing.

He could see from within that the dragonfly was a little girl trapped inside a body that she didn't feel was hers anymore. She didn't recognize herself or her family. She too was lost with no sense of belonging.

"Come sit with us," he said, "we can just be. You don't need to remember things when you are just being in the moment."

Chapter 5
The Throat Chakra - Space Element
"The space around us that allows the seeds to grow"

As the animals sat together there was a real sense of acceptance, understanding, respect and love between them.

"Thank you," said the dragonfly.

Before long they were joined by another forest friend, but again they had to have patience to allow her to join when she felt ready. The lion cub was ill, and with the treatment she was having to make her better she had lost all her fur. She was shy, as she came out from between the blades of grass to join the others.

Willow stood gently forwards reaching out to her and with no words between them they smiled to each other as she joined the group.

Once again, the animals sat in the sunlight enjoying the water from the flowers around.

There was no concept of time here, everything was much slower and peaceful with nowhere to go except be in the moment. Willow realised there was nothing to fear when in the present moment.

"Oh my, this is just wonderful," said Willow to the other animals.

"What is the wonderful feeling you have?" asked the humming bird.

"The voices in my head are silent," said Willow. "I hear nothing except the sound of the birds, the water and the beating of our hearts together. It's wonderful, I feel safe."

The sun began to fade and Willow began to hear a sound from deep within the forest as if it was calling to him again. He stood up, encouraging all his friends to follow.

The animals followed the calling and came to a river which sparkled and shimmered in the light of the new moon. The animals stood in amazement as the rippling colours of white, violet, blue, pink, yellow, orange and brown all swirled and connected together, rising from the water up towards the moon.

The colours all began to evaporate into the night sky bringing forward a new magic in the form of an animal lighting up the sky. With feathers like green and blue velvet a peacock appeared.

The humming bird dropped a blue crystal in Willow's paw and said to Willow that it was now time for a new message and the peacock began to share his message.

"I am here to remind you of your own light to shine. Embrace your uniqueness, it's what makes you special. Shine your light and let your weakness be the strength you show to others. Be proud of yourself for being you. Now dance together in the light of the moon. Be free, be you and give yourself love and kindness."

Chapter 6
The Third Eye Chakra – Light Element
"The source of light that allows the seeds to grow"

As the animals danced together in the moonlight... laughing and having fun, they felt free and accepted for being them... a feeling that went deeper than just fitting in... they had a sense of belonging.

Willow looked to the sky and softly said, "Thank you."

The moon was shining bright with no concept of time, her beautiful energy immortal and her love eternal.

After they danced, the animals all held hands and stood by the river edge, and before each of them shone the light of each of their reflections. Willow was confused when he looked as they all had two reflections looking back at them. The humming bird said, "Now it is time for your next message," and gave him an indigo coloured crystal

"What you see before you are the two reflections we each hold... our shadow self and our authentic true self."

Willow looked at the two bears looking back at him and didn't like looking at the darker bear with its shadow around it, he looked angry and sad. Willow no longer recognised his shadow bear; he had learned to let go of things in the forest.

His anger, his sadness, his resentment, his shame, his blame and his fear, but most importantly his false beliefs about himself. As he realised this his shadow bear reached out to him and gave him a clear stone before he began to disappear, then he was faced with the brightest bear he had ever seen... he was kind, caring, empathic, courageous and he felt such gratitude for his life and the love around him.

He had found his sense of belonging and his identity. He had nothing to fear, he had finally found the parts he was searching for: his love and acceptance of himself.

As Willow began to look at the reflections of his friend's they began, one by one, to disappear, and soon he was stood alone with only his own reflection and no one around. He called to the Humming bird but there was no reply.

Unsure where to turn once again he turned to the voices in his head, but this time with no feelings of fear or of not being good enough, he could trust this voice... this was his intuition.

The voice told Willow to look up and follow the star. Willow felt safe and began to follow the star and its light, walking back through the forest to where he began his journey, to the Weeping Willow Tree.

Chapter 7

The Crown Chakra – All Elements Together

"all elements together that allow the seeds to grow"

Willow noticed something small and glistening in the moonlight that was hanging from the tree branches that were now beginning to show leaves of emerald. He moved closer to investigate. Something felt familiar and was pulling him close. It was a chrysalis... it began to move.

"It's my caterpillar," he whispered softly to the tree, and just as he had with all his forest friend's, he waited until the caterpillar felt ready to show his wings. He knew in this moment as he waited that things were changing. Change didn't feel scary any more. He realised we need change to grow and learn, it's how we become who we are and mistakes are important too. This is where we learn the most.

He knew that with the love he felt inside that his caterpillar was ready to fly back to him. He closed his eyes and asked for a sign from his dad, and just as he had hoped, when he opened his eyes the most beautiful butterfly lay resting on his paw. He looked to the star in the sky and said, "Thank you."

As they sat together something inside surprised Willow as he looked to the butterfly with his wings softly fluttering as if trying to stay when he wanted to fly, "I have to let you go," he said, "its time, you need to fly, and I need to go back to where I belong."

The butterfly hovered just like the humming bird before him and said, "I have one final message before I go. You never gave up the hope of one day having the answers to all your questions, I have been listening all this time but I wanted to wait until I knew I had the life lessons and experience to answer. All the answers to your questions are just like being in the darkness of the chrysalis... like me, we were all once the caterpillar and when we find our wings to fly, we are never the same again."

The bear and his caterpillar shared their love in silence for their final few moments of being together and then in a blink of an eye... he flew away.

As Willow watched him soar slowly, he held his paws to his heart, smiled and whispered, "Thank you."

Afterword

"I believe that when faced with hardship or mental blocks, it's important to remember that there are always ways in which you can help the healing process. Friends and family are important too during these times and spending time doing things that make you feel happy always helps take you away from this negative frame of mind. Nobody should suffer in silence." - Jack Ramsay age 20

"In my mum's writing, the words made a very strong connection to me, it makes me think about how everyone you meet in life or cross paths with occurs for a reason and these people can help without realising it. Everyone has their own story and can still help, even if they need helped too. Life isn't always easy but no matter what it will always get better. Believe, hope and love everyone and everything in life." - Megan Ramsay age 19

"After reading, it made me reflect on how I felt when I was younger growing up, I felt just like Willow did before he met all the different animals just like I have met people, and friends now. Don't stop believing and losing faith because you are loved by people you might not even know or see, and there is always someone you can trust just like Willow's caterpillar". - Charlie Ramsay age 17

"In life sometimes we push people away that we don't mean to. The important thing is we don't reflect on that and be in the moment and don't see ourselves for who we were in the past. Accept who we are today because today is a new day" - Ava Ramsay age 9

After losing my partner to suicide in 2006 my journey with grief and that of my children has taken me to a place of love, compassion and strength where I want to help others. When I began writing this book I realised I hadn't fully let go of the feelings where I hadn't yet forgiven myself. I am sure as parents and carers we can all relate to that feeling of fear when have made mistakes despite trying our hardest to guide our children as best we can. It was only as I began to put pen to paper I realised something had changed within, because often we don't realise the weight of a feeling until we let it go.

Fifteen years ago I was a mum doing her best to survive loss after suicide with three young children. We can't get everything right and in grief I found that very hard to accept, I constantly feared my guidance wasn't good enough… only today do I realise forgiving Ross was never something I had to search for but forgiving myself has been a search I didn't even know I was looking for.

I would like to take this opportunity in my writing to thank my family, friends and also my clients… there is a little part of us all in Willow's journey.

A special mention to my Reiki Master's Elaine Dall, Louise Anderson and Carolanne Allardyce for all being a part of my spiritual journey and pushing me to believe in myself in the most gentle way.

About the Author

Lynsey Ramsay is a Soul Empowerment Coach, Counsellor and Angelic Reiki Master specialising in working with children and adults affected by grief, loss and trauma. She works from her studio Cherished Souls in Kirkcaldy, Fife, where she has created bespoke accredited training programmes which have been successfully integrated into schools and children's organisations.

CPSIA information can be obtained
at www.ICGtesting.com
Printed in the USA
BVHW021807191022
649833BV00008B/19